DOLPHIN'S
GRACE

DOLPHIN'S GRACE

AQUATIC ADVENTURES IN THE OVERWORLD
BOOK THREE

AN UNOFFICIAL MINECRAFTERS NOVEL

MAGGIE MARKS

Sky Pony Press
New York

AQUATIC ADVENTURES IN THE OVERWORLD: DOLPHIN'S GRACE.

Copyright © 2020 by Hollan Publishing, Inc.

Minecraft® is a registered trademark of Notch Development AB.
The Minecraft game is copyright © Mojang AB.

Sky Pony Press books may be purchased in bulk at special discounts for sales promotion, corporate gifts, fund-raising, or educational purposes. Special editions can also be created to specifications. For details, contact the Special Sales Department, Sky Pony Press, 307 West 36th Street, 11th Floor, New York, NY 10018 or info@skyhorsepublishing.com.

Sky Pony® is a registered trademark of Skyhorse Publishing, Inc.®, a Delaware corporation.

Visit our website at www.skyponypress.com.

10 9 8 7 6 5 4 3 2 1

Library of Congress Cataloging-in-Publication Data is available on file.

Special thanks to Erin L. Falligant.

Cover illustration by Amanda Brack
Cover design by Brian Peterson

Paperback ISBN: 978-1-5107-4731-9
E-book ISBN: 978-1-5107-4742-5

Printed in the United States of America

TABLE OF CONTENTS

DOLPHIN'S
GRACE

CHAPTER 1

Mason tugged on the oar, trying to propel the rowboat faster through the choppy water. But the boat felt so heavy!

He glanced at his little brother, who sat on a pile of prismarine blocks. They had mined the blocks at an ocean monument, but getting them home was tough work.

"Asher!" said Mason, nodding toward the oar at Asher's side. "Can I get a little help here?"

Asher didn't respond. He squinted into the sun. "Did you hear that?" he asked.

"What?" asked Mason, wiping a trickle of sweat from his brow.

"Dolphins!" cried Asher. He pointed.

Sure enough, a dolphin sprang from the water just beside Asher. It squealed and bobbed its short turquoise snout. Then, with a flick of its tail, it dove back into the waves.

Before Mason could speak, another dolphin popped out of the water only inches from his oar. It swam alongside the boat, dipping in and out of the water.

"It looks so . . . happy," Mason said, careful not to hit the dolphin with his paddle.

Asher leaned over to look. "It's smiling!" he cried.

It *did* look as if the dolphin were smiling. As two or three more of them darted and dove around the boat, Mason got the sense that the whole pod was playing— racing the boat to see who could get back to the underwater village first.

The dolphin in the lead seemed larger than the others, with a strong dorsal fin. "Is that one striped?" asked Mason, pointing.

As Asher leaned sideways trying to see, the boat rocked. A wave of water lapped over the side.

"Be careful!" Mason scolded.

Asher sat back, but he didn't take his eyes off the lead dolphin. "It's not stripes," he said. "It looks like . . . scars."

Mason's throat tightened. When the dolphin popped out of the water again, he saw its head and dorsal fin were crisscrossed with scars. It had battled something fierce—a drowned, maybe, with a sharp trident. And the dolphin had survived.

As it leaped out of the water, two more followed. Then another. And then another! Five dolphins dove in and out of the waves as if putting on a show.

"It's like they're playing Simon Says!" said Asher, laughing. "Simon is in the lead. And . . ." The smiley dolphin with the rounded snout leaped out of the water. "Happy is close behind!"

Mason laughed, too. Leave it to his little brother to start naming the dolphins as if they were pets.

When a third dolphin popped out of the water, it chirped and chattered, as if saying hello. "So what should we call this one?" asked Mason, pointing.

Asher reached out as if to stroke the dolphin's head. It gave one last squeal before ducking back underwater. "Squeaky," Asher announced. "That one has a *lot* to say." But he was leaning so far out of the boat, he wobbled. "Whoa!"

Mason grabbed Asher's green T-shirt and held on tightly, but Asher's helmet rolled out of his lap and plunked into the waves. Before Mason could grab it, a rounded snout knocked the helmet out of his reach.

"Give it back!" Asher cried, half-laughing and half-scolding.

The dolphins tossed the helmet back and forth like a ball. But as they darted farther and farther away from the boat, Mason's stomach sank. "You need that helmet," he reminded Asher. "We're out of potion of water breathing. The enchanted helmet is the only way you're going to be able to swim back home!"

Swim back home. The words still sounded strange. Mason and Asher had been sailing the ocean with their uncle. But when Uncle Bart was lost at sea, they'd made a new "home" with their friend Luna in the ruins of an underwater village. *And Luna's going to worry if we aren't back before sunset,* thought Mason, checking the horizon.

"I'll get the helmet," said Asher with a mischievous grin. "Watch me!"

Before Mason could grab him again, Asher dove off the edge of the boat.

"Asher, no!" Mason cried. But as he watched his brother swim with confident strokes after the pod of dolphins, he tried to relax. Asher had become a strong swimmer. And the dolphins weren't hostile mobs. Mason grabbed the oars and paddled after his brother.

When Asher reached the pod, they squeaked and squealed. They darted away from him and then back, as if curious about this new "fish" in the sea. He dove underwater, and when he surfaced, he had the helmet in his hand. "Got it!" he cried, holding it up like a trophy.

Suddenly, a square gray snout popped up out of the water and knocked the helmet out of Asher's hands.

"Hey! Give it back, Slugger!" he cried, diving after the dolphin. But "Slugger" got to the helmet first.

Mason stifled a smile as he watched his brother chase the dolphin. As the other dolphins swam alongside him, Asher suddenly had a burst of speed. He shot through the waves as if he were a dolphin himself, reaching the helmet before Slugger could take another whack at it.

"Yes!" Asher cried in victory. He didn't hold the helmet up in the air this time. Instead, he paddled quickly back toward the boat.

As Mason reached down to help his brother in, he whistled. "That was some pretty speedy swimming out there," he said. "You've gotten really good!"

Asher shrugged, but his cheeks pinked with pride. "I don't know what happened," he said. "All of a sudden, I felt like I could swim faster than any dolphin in the pod. Any dolphin in the ocean!"

A memory swam through Mason's mind—something Luna had said a few weeks ago. "Dolphin's Grace!" he reminded Asher. "If you swim close enough to the dolphins, you get a burst of speed. Luna told us about it, remember?"

Asher's green eyes widened. "Cool," he said. "We should try it again!"

Mason eyed the waves and caught sight of a few dolphin fins. The pod was still nearby. "Maybe," he said. "Let's get closer."

But as he took another strong stroke with his oar, it bumped into something. A fin shot out of the water, and the dolphin darted sideways with an upset squeal.

"What did you do?" asked Asher. "Did you hurt it?"

Mason swallowed hard. "I hope not. I think it's okay, see?" He watched the dolphin swim away.

But the other dolphins were swimming *toward* the boat. Simon, with his scarred dorsal fin, knocked against the hull.

"He's angry!" cried Asher, gripping the sides of the boat. "Because you hurt one of his pod."

Mason shook his head. "I didn't mean to. It was an accident!"

The dolphins circled the boat one last time, as if in warning. Then they took off with Simon in the lead. Mason watched the last fin disappear like a streak of silver in the setting sun.

"Great," Asher grumbled. "Way to ruin all the fun."

Mason sighed. "Sorry. But we have to get home anyway. Now help me paddle, would you? This prismarine weighs a ton."

With Asher's help, the boat began gliding forward again, toward the underwater village. But every few seconds, Mason checked the horizon, hoping to catch sight of the dolphins. Would they come back, or was that the last they'd see of the playful mobs?

CHAPTER 2

"Just one more!" Mason called to Asher.

They had anchored the boat next to a bubble column that led straight down to the underwater ruins. As Mason lifted the last block of prismarine from the boat, his arms ached. He hoisted it carefully over the side, trying to hand it to Asher, who waited in the water below. But Mason's fingers suddenly slipped—sending the block into the waves with a giant splash.

"Hey!" cried Asher, ducking out of the way. He swam toward the block and guided it toward the bubble column. *Glub, glub, glub* . . . The turquoise block disappeared.

Then Asher did, too, diving into the bubble column head first.

"Wait for—" Mason started to say. "Don't worry about it. I'll clean everything up." He sighed and gathered the things Asher had left behind in the boat: his pickaxe, a nautilus shell dropped by a drowned, and a bit of dried fish they'd brought to snack on.

Mason loaded up his backpack and jumped into the water, not even bothering to take a breath. The bubble column had all the oxygen he would need, at least until he hit the ocean floor.

The column sucked Mason downward at a dizzying pace. Bubbles brushed against his skin, and a school of pink tropical fish darted out of his path. Just before reaching bottom, Mason dove out of the column, avoiding the red-hot magma block at its base.

He nearly toppled over the pile of prismarine before catching his balance and adjusting his pack. Asher was swimming away—Mason could see the stream of bubbles his brother had left in his wake. But a dark-haired girl in a red shirt was swimming toward Mason. Luna!

As she eyed the pile of prismarine, she mouthed, "Wow." Then she reached for the top block and began to lug it toward the underwater village. Luna never wasted time when there was work to be done.

Mason grabbed a block and swam after her, until he realized he could move more quickly by *walking* on the ocean floor with the heavy block. Even underwater, where everything felt lighter, the block still weighed him down.

As the fields of sea grass and kelp gave way to moss-covered sandstone, the underwater village came into view. Mason lugged the prismarine block beneath a crumbling stone arch, past a sandstone wall with a sleepy squid hovering near its top, and toward a stone "castle" with mossy cobblestone steps.

As Luna and Mason passed the castle, the world ahead brightened, lit by the conduit they had built. Like a beacon, the conduit lit up the ocean floor—and made it a whole lot safer, too. Anyone swimming near the conduit could breathe underwater, see more clearly, and mine more quickly. But hostile mobs were hurt by the conduit, so they stayed away.

The conduit was Asher's idea, Mason remembered. Well, actually it had been Uncle Bart's idea—a diagram sketched into his old leather journal. *But I'm going to help Asher make it bigger and better. Even if we have to carry a* hundred *blocks of prismarine!* Mason jutted out his chin and hoisted the heavy block higher.

Luna was already adding her block to the frame, building a new ring around the conduit like a ribbon around a package. With every extra ring, the conduit would become more powerful. Soon its protective glow would stretch out past the sandstone castle, all the way to the kelp farm near the bubble column. Maybe even farther!

Excitement trickled down Mason's spine. As he placed his prismarine block next to Luna's, he gazed at the glowing blue orb spinning inside the conduit. He closed his eyes and listened to the *thump, thump, thump* coming from the contraption like a reassuring heartbeat. As he rested his hand on the frame, he felt a vibration run from his head to his toes.

Mason opened his eyes and turned back toward the bubble column. There were a gazillion more prismarine blocks to lug across the ocean floor. But where was Asher? His redheaded brother had a way of wiggling out of work.

Sure enough, Asher was swimming up above, doing somersaults. Mason was about to wave him down when he saw a flicker of movement nearby. A drowned? His hand darted toward the handle of his trident.

No—the creature swimming toward Asher was friendly. And familiar. A dolphin!

Up ahead, Luna stopped swimming and gazed at the creature too, a smile spreading across her face.

Dolphins didn't usually swim this close to the underwater village. But lately, they'd been curious and had come nosing around. *Because of the conduit,* Mason realized. The conduit had made the village a safe place for dolphins and fish to swim without running into hostile mobs.

Asher waved to get Mason's attention. He pointed toward another dolphin hovering near the glass walls of the brothers' underwater home. Even from a few yards away, Mason recognized the scarred dorsal fin. It was *Simon.* This was the same pod of dolphins that had swum alongside the boat earlier!

A wave of relief washed over Mason. Had the dolphins forgiven him for bumping one of their pod mates with a paddle? He hoped so.

He counted to be sure they were all there: *One, two, three, four . . . five. Yes!* Mason recognized Happy, who swam past with a smile. Turquoise-colored Squeaky dove low toward Luna, chirping a greeting. And Slugger was there too, balancing a tiny turtle shell on his nose.

As a fourth dolphin with a long snout somersaulted through the water, Luna swam up to greet it.

She circled the pod, quick as lightning. Had she taken a swig of potion of swiftness? *No,* Mason realized. *It's Dolphin's Grace!* Luna had gotten a burst of speed by swimming with the dolphins, just as Asher had earlier.

Mason's limbs itched to swim toward the pod—to join Asher and Luna in the game and to feel Dolphin's Grace, even for a few seconds. As he swam toward Luna, she spun in the water and greeted him with a smile. But the moment he reached her side, Simon squealed as if calling out a warning. The dolphin shot toward the water's surface, and his pod mates followed—without even a head bob or tail flick goodbye.

Luna watched them go, confusion on her face. But when Asher swam closer, Mason could see the angry furrow of his brow. He pointed at Mason as if to say, *You did it again! Why do you keep scaring off the dolphins?*

I don't know! Mason wanted to cry. He drifted back down to the ocean floor like a deflated pufferfish. But when his feet touched bottom, he stood up straight. There was still work to be done—more prismarine blocks to move.

He headed back along the coral-lined reef toward the bubble column. When a shadow caught his eye, he glanced up and saw Asher swimming toward him.

Asher held out his hand, showing off the tiny turtle shell Slugger had been playing with. Except it *wasn't* a turtle shell. It was an emerald!

Mason did a double take. The gem caught the light of the conduit, casting a spray of green sparkles into the water. Mason raised his arms as if to ask, *Where'd you get that?*

Asher made a swimming motion with his hand and pointed upward, where the dolphins had swum away.

Had they given him a gift?

CHAPTER 3

"Where do you think Slugger found an emerald?" Asher asked, admiring the treasure in his hands. The gem seemed especially shiny now that they were in Luna's underwater home, warming themselves by the furnace.

Luna wrung the water out of her dark ponytail. "I heard dolphins know how to find buried treasure," she said, her eyes gleaming.

Uh-oh, thought Mason. Luna had just said the two magic words—the ones that would make Asher go bonkers and forget everything else. *Buried treasure.*

Mason swallowed hard. To hunt buried treasure, Asher might have to leave the safety of the conduit. Face hostile mobs. And maybe not return at all. *Just like Uncle Bart.*

"How do I get them to lead me to the treasure?" Asher asked, sitting up straight.

Luna shrugged. "Earn their trust, I guess."

"But how?"

Mason tried to change the subject—fast. "I'll tell you how *not* to earn the dolphins' trust," he joked. "Accidentally bump one with a paddle, and they'll never forgive you."

"Huh?" Luna said.

He explained what had happened in the boat. "That's why they all disappeared when I tried to swim with you just now," he said.

Luna shrugged. "They were probably just going up for a breath of air," she said.

"Air?" Asher said. "Dolphins don't need to breathe!"

"Sure, they do," Luna said. "They need water to survive, but they also need air. They go up to the water's surface every few minutes for a quick breath."

Asher scratched his nose. "Huh. I didn't know that."

For just a moment, Mason thought his brother had forgotten about the buried treasure. Then Asher glanced down again at the emerald. "I'm going to earn the dolphins' trust," he announced. "If I have to swim and play with them every day—*all* day. If dolphins can lead me to treasure, who needs buried treasure maps?"

He laughed and stuck the emerald in his pocket, as if he'd just discovered the secret to happiness. Then he left the furnace room whistling.

As Mason watched his brother go, his stomach sank. If Asher was on the hunt for more treasure, there would be no stopping him.

* * *

The next morning, as Mason stacked prismarine blocks in a third ring around the conduit, Asher swam with the dolphins.

And played.

And swam.

And played some more.

Mason tried to ignore the circus going on overhead, partly because he didn't want to scare the dolphins away again—and partly because he was mad at Asher. *Why do I have to build a more powerful conduit all by myself?* he grumbled. *This was Asher's idea in the first place. He should help me!*

But Luna wasn't even helping anymore. She had gone fishing for lunch, taking her fishing pole and a bucket and heading toward a patch of sea grass on the far end of the coral reef.

When she finally came back, her bucket heavy with fish, Asher swam to greet her.

Sure, thought Mason. *Now he thinks he can get a free lunch.*

Then he remembered: Asher would *never* eat raw fish. He'd only recently learned to eat cooked fish, mostly because a boy can't live on dried kelp alone. So why was Asher taking a raw codfish out of the bucket?

As he swam back toward the pod with the fish, Mason realized Asher was going to feed the dolphins! But would they eat the fish he offered?

Asher waved the floppy codfish in the water until the pod swam closer. Then one dolphin—the unnamed one with the long snout—darted forward and snatched the fish right out of his hand.

Squeaky chided her hungry pod mate with a few chirps, and Simon bumped against the dolphin as if to say, *Don't be so greedy!*

When Luna offered Asher more fish, he took four—enough to feed the rest of the pod. And soon they were circling around him, eager for more.

Luna emptied her bucket, giving Asher the last fat fish. This one he offered only to Simon.

Smart, Mason thought. If there was one dolphin whose trust Asher needed to win, it was the leader of the pod.

Simon ate the fish and instantly darted away. But why? Mason's heart thudded in his ears. *Did I somehow scare them away again?* he wondered.

Asher watched in confusion too as the whole pod began to swim away. Then Simon circled back around, as if to say, *Follow us!*

Asher didn't waste a second. He took off after the pod so quickly that Mason could tell his brother had received another boost of Dolphin's Grace.

Then Mason realized something else: If the dolphins were leading Asher to buried treasure, how far would he have to swim? How far *could* he swim? Asher wouldn't be able to breathe past the safety of the conduit; not for very long, anyway.

As he disappeared around a rocky outcropping, Mason started to panic. If Asher thought the dolphins were leading him to treasure, he'd never turn around. He would swim straight into danger!

Mason pushed off from the ocean floor and swam, kicking furiously. He had to catch up with his brother.

In the light of the conduit, he saw Asher swimming ahead through the underwater ruins of the village. Faster than fast, he wound around the crumbly castle walls.

Mason took long, strong strokes, trying to build some speed of his own. But the world was growing dimmer now. With every stroke, he was moving away from the conduit. Soon, he wouldn't be able to see anything. Or breathe.

Panic gripped his chest. He swam through the window of a sandstone wall and kicked off from the structure, yearning for more speed.

Asher, stop! he wanted to cry.

But now he couldn't see his brother at all.

CHAPTER 4

Mason scanned the shadowy ruins of the underwater village, desperate to spot some sign of
Asher. Stalks of kelp swayed in the current,
catching Mason's eye. He spun around to get a better
look at . . . the tentacles of a squid dangling near a tree
of coral. But where was Asher?

The answer came in a flurry of bubbles.

Someone swam back toward Mason from the darkness beyond the conduit. Asher!

He didn't stop to say hello. He burst past, as if still
under the spell of the Dolphin's Grace. Except this
time, he wasn't trying to keep up with the dolphins.
The pod was nowhere in sight.

He must be out of breath, Mason realized. *He's trying
to get back to the conduit!* Mason's own lungs burned.
He kicked hard to follow his brother back toward the
light.

When they reached the safety of the conduit, Asher
kept going. He swam to the dirt mound that hid the

entrance to their house and sped through the first door, nearly closing it on Mason.

Mason pushed through the door behind Asher and then pulled the door shut. They waited for the sponge mat at their feet to absorb the water from the world beyond the door. Then they pushed through the second entrance into the dark, dry foyer of their home.

Here, finally, Mason could scold Asher for swimming so far away. For chasing the dolphins without making a plan. "How could you—" he began.

"I lost them!" Asher interrupted. "They were leading me to treasure. I know they were! But I lost them." He balled his hands into fists.

Mason sighed. "C'mon," he said, leading his brother down the long hall that opened into brightness. They had added a second room to the house, this one made of tinted blue glass. From the village outside, the glass was nearly invisible. Fish and squid bumped into the walls sometimes, as if they thought they could swim right through. Here, the light of the conduit shone bright, and Mason instantly felt safer—and calmer.

He dried off with a towel and tossed one to Asher, too. Then he said, more kindly this time, "You never would have made it to the treasure, Asher. You didn't have a potion of water breathing, or an enchanted helmet. How were you planning to *breathe*?"

Asher's green eyes widened. He scowled, then shrugged. "That's beside the point," he muttered. "I lost the dolphins because they were too fast."

Mason cocked his head. "But what about Dolphin's

Grace? I saw how fast you were swimming! Way faster than Luna—and she's lived down here so long, she's practically a fish."

Asher sighed. "Dolphin's Grace doesn't last very long—only like five seconds. So if I'm going to find that treasure, I'm going to need potion of swiftness, and boots enchanted with Depth Strider. I'm going to need . . ."

"Luna?" Mason suggested. Their friend Luna was a master potion brewer. Plus, she had found an old anvil in the basement of the crumbly sandstone castle in the village, so now she could enchant armor and weapons, too.

Asher blew out his breath. "Yep, I'm going to need Luna."

No sooner had the words left his mouth than the brothers heard a thump at their front door. Mason's heart skipped a beat. Not long ago, that thumping sound could have been a drowned, a hostile mob that had threatened to take over the underwater world here at the ocean's floor.

The drowned are gone, he reminded himself. *Because of the conduit. That's just Luna coming to check on Asher.* Or it was Luna's pet squid Edward, who sometimes appeared at their window, begging for a piece of raw fish.

Thump, thump . . . tha-thump, thump, thump.

Nope, this was definitely Luna. Mason grinned and jogged down the hall. He opened the inner door to find a very wet Luna standing on the bloated sponge mat.

"Did Asher come back?" she asked. She was still holding her empty fish bucket. When she noticed Mason's eyes on it, she gave an embarrassed laugh. "Sorry, I should have left this outside. I was afraid that dolphin—what do you call him, Slugger?—would turn this into his newest toy." She set down the bucket and hurried down the hall, poking her head into the living room. "Asher!"

By the time Mason reached them, Asher was already giving Luna a list of what he would need for his next outing with the dolphins. "Potions of water breathing, night vision, and swiftness. Boots enchanted with Depth Strider. Oh, and plenty of raw fish for keeping the dolphins happy."

Mason shot him a look. "I'm pretty sure you can catch your own fish," he said.

Asher shrugged. "Yeah, you're right. But we'd better hurry." He swung his head to stare out the glass window. "The pod could be back any minute now!"

When he sprang out of his chair, Mason held up a hand to stop him. "That treasure isn't going anywhere," he reminded his brother. "And I could use your help finding more prismarine blocks before you go."

"The treasure *might* go somewhere, if someone else finds it first," Asher pointed out. His cheeks flushed at the thought of missing out on that treasure.

Suddenly, he held up a finger, as if he'd just had a brilliant idea. "Besides, I might find prismarine crystals in that buried treasure chest! And you know what that means?"

Mason sighed. "No, but I'm pretty sure you're going to tell me."

"You can craft *sea lanterns* with prismarine crystals," Asher announced.

Mason scratched his head. "Yeah, so?"

Asher gave an exasperated sigh, as if Mason were the dumbest zombie in the pit. "You can use sea lanterns in place of prismarine for the conduit frame, right?"

Mason shook his head. "It's a lot easier to find prismarine blocks than to craft sea lanterns out of prismarine crystals."

Asher shrugged. "Well, maybe I like to be creative. And maybe I *don't* like lugging heavy blocks all the way here from the ocean monuments where we find them."

Mason couldn't argue with that, as much as he wanted to. His arms were still sore from carrying the last batch of blocks. He blew out his breath. "All right, so you're going treasure hunting. But you're not going alone. Let me do a little more work on the conduit tomorrow, and then we'll go the next day. Deal?"

Asher stared at the glass ceiling, chewing on that thought. Finally, he held out his hand. "Deal."

Luna gave a long, low whistle. "Phew! I'm glad that's settled. Guess I have some potions to brew." She turned on her heel to head back home. "Come find me tonight, Asher," she called over her shoulder. "I'll have everything ready, okay?"

But Asher was already gone, rummaging through the supply chests in the furnace room.

Mason locked eyes with Luna and shrugged. When Asher was on a mission, there was no stopping him.

So I'm going to have to get ready, too. Ready for another adventure.

He shrugged off a niggle of worry and followed Asher down the hall.

*   *   *

Mason woke to sunlight filtering through the glass ceiling of his bedroom.

He stretched, wincing at the soreness of his shoulders and arms. *Just one more day of lifting prismarine blocks,* he reminded himself. Then he and Asher would be chasing dolphins toward buried treasure. Mason shook his head. *What do I let Asher get me into?* He rolled out of bed and reached for his khaki pants.

Squeak, squeak. The sound stopped him in his tracks, his hand freezing midair. What was that? Silverfish?

He scanned the room, remembering the small critters he and his uncle had found in a cave once while searching for treasure. Uncle Bart was *always* looking for treasure, just like Asher. But sometimes what he found instead were hostile mobs—or *annoying* ones, like silverfish.

Chirp, chirp, squeak. The sound came from the

other side of the glass. Mason craned his neck to see beyond the edge of the dirt mound.

There! A dolphin's tail disappeared around the mound. Had Squeaky come to pay them a morning visit?

The noisy dolphin wouldn't be traveling alone. Mason checked through the glass again, this time looking the other way. Sure enough, the pod was back.

Happy smiled into the sunlight filtering through the water. Slugger nudged playfully at Simon's side until Simon pushed him away with his snout. And the dolphin that Asher now called "Hungry"—the one who had gobbled his raw cod in one bite—was nosing around the bottom of the ocean floor, as if looking for breakfast.

When a swimmer appeared, Hungry darted toward him. Mason recognized Asher's red hair peeking out from beneath his iron helmet. But what was Asher doing outside this early? And . . . why was he wearing his helmet? He didn't need it here—not with the conduit nearby, which gave anyone swimming near it the water breathing effect.

Mason rubbed his eyes. Then a thought struck. *Asher's wearing his helmet because he's leaving. He's going to search for buried treasure—without me!*

Mason rapped on the glass, willing his brother to stop or to at least turn his head. But Asher was too busy feeding Simon a hunk of cod. When Simon took off, calling his pod to follow with a sharp squeal, Asher followed too.

Mason watched his brother shoot along the coral reef, boosted by Dolphin's Grace. When the pod swam over a rocky ridge, Asher followed.

Then he was gone.

CHAPTER 5

Mason had never dressed so quickly. By the time he reached the supply chest, he'd managed to get his arms into his turquoise shirt, but the back of the shirt was where the front should be. He scowled and pulled it off again.

Then he rummaged through the supply chest to see what was missing—what Asher had taken with him. The fishing rod was gone, along with Asher's pickaxe. Uncle Bart's iron helmet was missing, the one engraved with the letter *B*. And the stash of potions that Luna had given the boys was a whole lot smaller now—just a few squat bottles with orange corks and colorful liquid sloshing inside.

Mason didn't know whether to be alarmed or relieved. Asher had gone off on his own, but at least he'd taken armor and potions with him, along with a pickaxe that could *sort of* be used as a weapon.

Mason quickly closed the chest. There was no way

he could catch up with his brother now. So what could he do?

Find Luna, came the answer in his head. *She'll know what to do.*

*   *   *

"Aren't you even the slightest bit worried?" Mason asked again, throwing out his arms.

Luna chewed her lip. "Sure," she said. "But Asher is a treasure hunter, so . . . we're going to have to let him hunt treasure. And I'll help you with the conduit. We'll head to the monument to get more prismarine, and by the time we get back, Asher will be back, too—you'll see." She gave him a reassuring smile.

Mason couldn't muster one up in return, not until Luna promised to enchant his pickaxe with Efficiency to make mining a whole lot faster and easier.

Before he knew it, they were leaving the safety of the conduit, just as Asher had. Except instead of swimming, Luna and Mason took the rowboat, hoping to bring back a load of turquoise blocks.

As he rowed the boat toward the ocean monument, Mason scanned the waves, searching for fins. Would the dolphins come back soon? And would Asher be with them? Mason's heart thumped hopefully in his chest.

Soon the boat was gliding over the ocean monument. The sprawling pyramid stretched out below, a huge square building flanked by two long wings. Mason rowed toward the back of the monument, avoiding the front entrance. Guardians lurked there. The hostile fish-like mobs lurked *everywhere*. But Mason was getting to know the monument now—where prismarine could be mined easily, and where danger was sure to strike.

"Here?" Luna asked, gesturing toward the water below.

Mason nodded and threw the anchor over the edge of the boat. Then he reached for his weapon: a trident Luna had enchanted with Riptide. If he threw the weapon, it would propel him forward through the water, which could help him escape hostile mobs. *Can it help me get the prismarine blocks up to the rowboat, too?* he wondered. It was worth a shot.

Luna's own trident was enchanted with loyalty, which meant it came back to her after every throw. She had also packed potions. "Drink up," she told Mason, handing him the first bottle.

He swallowed the potions one by one—potion of swiftness, potion of night vision, and potion of water breathing. Only the last one tasted horrible, like pufferfish, slime, and fermented spider eyes all rolled into one. Mason never asked Luna what was in her potions—he didn't want to know. He just plugged his nose and forced himself to swallow.

While he waited for the potions to kick in, he tightened his turtle shell helmet on his head. It would help him breathe underwater a little longer if Luna's potion of water breathing ran out. As he grabbed his pickaxe, he thought again of Asher.

What if the dolphins led Asher to a cave that he had to mine his way through? What if it was dark inside, and mobs spawned, and Asher was there all alone?

When Luna snapped her fingers in front of his face, Mason leaned backward, rocking the boat.

"What?" he asked. "Why'd you do that?"

"I asked if you were ready," said Luna. "Three times. Are the potions starting to work?"

Mason stared at the water below. The potion of night vision had definitely kicked in. He could see the ocean monument more clearly now—the outline of each prismarine brick and block. Maybe mining would help him forget about Asher for a while. He nodded at Luna, climbed over the edge of the boat, and plunged into the waves.

The chill of the water gave way to warmth as Mason began to swim, quick as lightning with the potion of swiftness. *Is this what Dolphin's Grace feels like?* he wondered.

As he neared the back of the monument, he noticed every detail of the prismarine—aqua blue blocks flecked with dark green and yellow. He swam toward a window in the wall, just large enough to fit through. After doing a quick check for guardians, he paddled through the window into a long hallway lit by sea lanterns.

When he saw that Luna had swum into the hall safely behind him, he began to mine. *Clink, clink, clink!* It took several whacks at the prismarine to force a block out of the wall.

Again, Mason thought of Asher, wishing his little brother were here to help—wishing he didn't have to worry about him *all* the time. With each whack at the wall, Mason grew more worried. And tired. And frustrated.

Even if Asher were here, he wouldn't be helping, Mason decided. Asher would be trying to tunnel into the treasure chamber of the monument to get the gold blocks. Or he'd be fighting guardians to collect their drops. Any treasure at all was worth seeking out, as far as Asher was concerned.

Whack, whack, whack! Mason swung so hard, his shoulders shook.

Someone was squeezing his arm now—probably Luna, telling him to slow down and pace himself. But Mason didn't want to.

Thwack, thwack, thwack!

Another block fell out of the wall, nearly landing on his toes. He leaped backward, right into Luna. This time she grabbed his arm and didn't let go. Mason swung his head around to find out why.

Her mouth was set in a firm line. She pointed.

He followed her gaze down the hall and saw the guardian lurking in the shadows, its spiky thorns extended and its single eye staring—directly at Mason.

Any moment now, the fish-like beast would charge.

Then, with a thrash of its barbed tail, it did.

CHAPTER 6

A shot of energy ran from Mason's head to his toes. As the guardian lunged toward him, Mason swung his pickaxe. There was no time to grab his trident. No time to dodge the mob or swim away. Only time to fight.

As Mason's axe struck, the beast released an angry growl. It tumbled sideways and sank. Then, glowing red with rage, it righted itself and charged again.

Something streaked through the water beside Mason—something shiny. Luna's trident struck the scaly beast in the side, knocking it back. The mob grunted and thrashed, trying to free itself of the weapon.

When Luna held out her hand, her trident shot back through the water, straight into her fist.

The Loyalty enchantment! Mason remembered.

Then he remembered his own weapon, enchanted with Riptide. He dropped the pickaxe and grabbed the trident strapped to his waist. Before the guardian could recover from Luna's blow, Mason delivered one of his own. He swung his arm back and sent the trident through the water like a spear. Mason sailed through the water behind it.

He was beside the guardian in a flash, ready to swing his trident again like a sword. He watched, waiting for the beast to rise, but . . . the guardian grunted and was gone.

Mason searched the hall for Luna. She had swum to the far end, as if looking for more hostile mobs. When she caught Mason's eye, she gave him a thumbs-up, the all-clear sign.

Except it wasn't.

Mason saw the shadows lurking behind her. More spikes. More thorns. More guardians.

He waved wildly to warn her, but it was too late! In a flash of purple, one of the guardians fired its laser. Luna lurched forward, struck from behind. Her eyes widened with fear, and she dropped her trident.

Do something! Mason urged himself. But he couldn't throw his trident—Luna was in the way! So he did the only thing he could do. He charged.

Mason swam as if his own life depended on it, whipping through the water like a guardian itself. He pushed Luna to safety and then whirled around to face the thorned beasts.

They were so close now, Mason could reach out and touch them. He swung his trident side to side, counting the beasts as he battled them. *One, two, three* . . . could he take them all down before one of them fired?

With a grunt and a growl, one mob dropped. Mason didn't wait for it to pop back up. He struck the next, plunging his trident into the mob's fleshy side. It took all his strength to pull the weapon back out.

The beast raged, red hot with anger. But Mason kept fighting. He swung his trident until his shoulders went numb. Until the hall darkened, and his limbs felt heavy.

The potions are wearing off! he realized. Which meant soon, he and Luna wouldn't be able to breathe.

He glanced backward to make sure she was okay. Luna was pushing herself to her feet, leaning against the prismarine wall for support. She locked eyes with him and pointed toward the window, the one that led to safety—back up to the rowboat.

Mason gave the third guardian one last blast with his trident. Then he waited, willing the beast to stay down.

It did. In a stream of bubbles, Mason blew out the breath he'd been holding.

The hallway was empty now, except for the guardian drops: a few prismarine shards. *Asher might care about those,* thought Mason, *but I don't.*

He ignored the drops and quickly swam to Luna's side. Together they half-walked, half-swam toward the light of the window. As they passed the pile of prismarine blocks they had mined, Mason hesitated. Could they leave the blocks behind? Their hard work would be wasted!

But one look at Luna's pale face gave him the answer he needed. Luna needed to get to safety—fast.

He pushed her through the window first. Then he wrapped an arm around her and used his other hand to throw his trident toward the boat. The Riptide enchantment propelled Mason through the water, taking Luna up to the surface, too.

She moved more easily now. She gripped the edge of the boat and pulled while Mason pushed. Together, they made their way into the boat. Then Luna flopped into the hull like a fish in a bucket.

Mason sucked cool air into his lungs and sat back, staring at the blue sky above.

"Thanks," Luna finally whispered. "I'm sorry about the prismarine."

Mason shrugged. "No worries." He glanced back into the water, wondering if there was time to go back for some of the blocks. But he would have to go alone.

Alone like Asher, he suddenly realized. *What if Asher runs into guardians? Who will pull him to safety?*

Mason shivered as he reached for the oars.

* * *

Back home, Mason paced.

Luna had been wrong. Asher *wasn't* home when they returned from the ocean monument.

He wasn't home at dinnertime, when Mason cooked extra kelp and fish in the furnace, just in case. And as the sky darkened high above the ocean floor, even the light of the conduit couldn't keep Mason's fear at bay.

Finally, when he couldn't stand it anymore, he left the glass walls of his underground home and swam toward Luna's. Sea lanterns lit the path along the rocky ridge, and there—in the sea grass near the entrance—Edward the Squid lay resting. But Mason barely stopped to say hello.

He brushed the squid's smooth head with his hand and swam overhead, straight into the tunnel bored into the rock. The tunnel was so tight! Months ago, Mason had been scared to swim through it. Now he knew that if he pushed his way toward the light at the end, he would be there in no time. He burst into the lantern-lit room and dried off with the sea sponge before knocking on Luna's inner door.

"Asher isn't back yet!" The words burst out of Mason's mouth before Luna could even greet him.

She waved him inside. But why was she smiling?

"Don't worry," she said brightly. "Look!" She pointed through the glass wall of her living room.

Mason saw nothing. He crossed the room in a flash and looked through the window. "What?"

"There!" she insisted, pointing again.

Something swam near the conduit. Mason squinted to see. It was a dolphin. A dolphin! "They're back!" he cried.

One by one, the pod swam into view. But Simon wasn't in the lead. Was that Happy? Mason couldn't tell. The dolphin's rounded snout didn't look particularly smiley tonight.

Gray Slugger swam close behind, right past the fish bucket resting on the frame of the conduit. The dolphin didn't bother to nudge the bucket with his nose. *Why not?* Mason wondered.

Turquoise-colored Squeaky brought up the rear. But . . . where were the other two dolphins? Where were Simon and Hungry?

And where is Asher? Mason pressed closer to the glass, craning his neck to search the ocean behind Squeaky. Clear blue water stretched out for yards.

Mason watched and waited, until his palms began to sweat. "Where's my brother?" he cried. "Where's Asher?"

Luna searched, too. She ran to the other pane of glass, as if Asher might have circled around toward the front door. Mason held his breath, hoping she would have good news, but Luna just shook her head sadly.

When something bumped the glass, Mason whirled around and came face to face with a dolphin. Squeaky nudged the glass again with its snout and began chattering excitedly.

"What does it want?" Mason asked.

Luna crossed the floor and studied the dolphin. It squeaked and squealed, swimming away from the glass and then back.

"Squeaky is trying to tell us something," Luna murmured under her breath. "Something's wrong."

Mason's stomach dropped. But he'd known it

already—he knew it the second the dolphins came back without their leader, and without Asher.

Asher was in trouble.

CHAPTER 7

"**T**hey want us to follow them!" said Luna, her face pressed against the glass.

All three dolphins were chattering now, swimming near the glass wall and then flipping around and swimming away.

Mason was already pulling on his boots. He reached for his helmet and trident. "Let's go!"

"Wait!" Luna said. "We need to pack potions. We don't know how far away we'll have to swim."

She sounds like me, Mason realized. *The way I sounded when Asher wanted to follow the dolphins to buried treasure.* But that was *before*—before Asher was in trouble. Now all Mason wanted to do was fly out the front door and follow the pod, wherever they might lead.

Luna forced him to wait, just long enough to drink a few potions. And then they were stepping out into the cool water, searching for the dolphins.

Squeaky showed up first. With a squeal and an excited flip of its tail, the dolphin swam near. But when Mason reached out his hand in greeting, the dolphin quickly swam away.

They still don't trust me! Mason realized sadly. *I'm still scaring the dolphins away.*

Luna was prepared for that. She pulled wrapped fish from her pack and offered Mason a slippery hunk of raw cod. He grabbed hold of it and held it out.

Squeaky circled Mason, chattering all the while, but the dolphin wouldn't eat the fish. Happy and Slugger didn't even come near. They hovered in the distance, watching warily.

Take it! Mason wanted to cry. He waved the fish in the water. *Take it and lead me to my brother!*

Finally, he tossed the fish back to Luna. Maybe they would trust her. Maybe she could work her magic, and they'd start swimming already.

Sure enough, as soon as Luna held the fish, the dolphins darted in, ready for a bite. She fed them all, and even stroked Happy's snout, before the pod turned and began to swim.

Mason swallowed his disappointment. *It doesn't matter if they trust me,* he told himself. *What matters is that they take me to Asher. Now!*

The pod of dolphins—and Luna—took off like a shot. Dolphin's Grace had struck again. *But not for me,* Mason realized. He stroked his way through the water, desperate to catch up. Even with potion of swiftness, he passed the conduit, the sandstone castle, and the bubble column way behind the others.

Leaving the safety of the underwater village, he trailed Luna, keeping an eye on her red shirt and the flash of her trident. Without Simon, their leader, the dolphins swam in a scattered formation. Who was leading the pack? Slugger tried, but Happy and Squeaky passed by, each taking a turn. Every few minutes, the dolphins rose to the water's surface, where Luna was swimming.

She's avoiding the drowned, Mason realized. Here, away from the conduit, they would soon encounter hostile mobs. But if they stayed near the surface, where sunlight filtered in from the sky above, the drowned might leave them alone. The hostile mobs would hover along the ocean floor, where the light couldn't reach. *At least, I hope they will,* thought Mason with a quick glance over his shoulder.

Now they were nearing the ocean monument, its prismarine pillars rising all around. Mason's heart pounded in his ears as he remembered the guardian attack he and Luna had survived just a few hours ago. The dolphins gave the monument a wide berth, as if they feared the guardians too. They picked up their speed, which meant Mason had to work twice as hard to keep up.

He set his sights on Luna's shirt, blocking out everything else, and just swam. *Stroke, kick, stroke, kick, stroke, kick . . .*

Finally, they'd passed the monument, and the pod slowed their pace. They drifted downward toward a coral reef, toward the safety of a kelp forest and some crumbling underwater ruins. Mason glanced ahead, wondering if Luna would leave the water's surface and follow the pod. What if Asher were down there, trapped in the ruins of an underwater castle?

Luna must have had the same thought, because she dove low, surprising a school of tiny purple fish. Mason followed, feeling the tickle of sea grass against his arms and legs. His heart began to slow, and for just a moment, he gave his limbs a rest. He stroked the water instead of furiously carving through it.

Then he thought of Asher. *He's in trouble! There's no time to rest!* Mason kicked forward to see where the dolphins were leading him, hoping they knew where Asher was—and could get to him in time.

Mason swam past Luna, who had paused to take another swig of potion. He swam past Slugger, who seemed way too interested in a nautilus shell on the ocean floor. Happy and Squeaky were leading the pod, side by side—until Squeaky made a dramatic turn to the left.

With a squeal of warning, the dolphin darted back past Mason toward Luna. Happy followed.

Wait! Mason wanted to cry out. *Why are you going backward? Asher needs us!*

Then he saw.

Along the coral reef ahead, a tall clump of sea grass shivered and shook. Something stepped out—a staggering green mob with tattered brown clothing.

It growled, its eerie blue eyes glowing in the murky waters.

As Mason grabbed his weapon, he spotted something in the hostile mob's hand. The drowned had spawned with a trident! And it was about to launch it. Mason darted sideways, hoping Luna wasn't close behind. He turned to warn her. But the drowned's trident didn't strike Luna—not even close. It zoomed past her surprised face and struck the dolphin swimming behind her.

Slugger! The weapon stuck in the dolphin's side. It thrashed its tail fin, trying to dislodge it. Slugger rolled through the water while Squeaky circled round, squealing with fear.

Mason froze, torn between helping the injured dolphin and battling the undead mob.

The drowned made the choice for him, because the mob's outstretched hands suddenly held another weapon. Another trident. But how?

There was no time to wonder. Mason launched his own trident, hitting the drowned square in the chest. It staggered backward and released its weapon. That gave Mason the time he needed to swim forward—to retrieve his trident and swing it again.

Thwack, thwack, thwack!

Then he saw the other drowned—three or four of them, rising out of the kelp like an army.

I'm outnumbered! Mason realized, his chest tight. He whirled around, looking for Luna. She swam near

Slugger holding two tridents—her own, and the bloody one she had just pulled from the dolphin's side.

Mason waved her forward. *There's more!* he tried to tell her. *Look!*

The moment Luna saw the drowned, her eyes widened. But before she could release her trident or swim toward Mason, something else did—a pod of angry dolphins. *They're turning on the drowned just like they turned on me!* Mason thought, remembering the moment when he had accidentally hit one with his paddle.

Squeaky soared past Mason, knocking the first drowned backward with its snout. Happy knocked the second off its feet. And then Slugger came too, bleeding from his side, but charging forward with an angry squeal.

Mason didn't wait for another dolphin to be injured. He swam straight into the army of drowned, waving his trident wildly. The mobs snarled. One slashed at Mason with its own weapon. He ducked and darted back in, scarcely breathing, until the mob dropped with an angry grunt.

Thwack, thwack! Mason battled another hostile mob to the ground. And then another. Rotten flesh sizzled, sending tiny bubbles upward.

Were they gone? Mason spun around, searching for more drowned, as the dolphins circled overhead. Luna was beside him, her chest heaving. She nodded at Mason as if to say, *Let's go. Let's not wait for more to spawn.*

Back to the water's surface they swam, high enough that Mason could pop his head out into the sunshine and take a gulp of air—real air. When he did, Happy burst from the water ahead of him. The dolphin soared through the air, smiling. Squeaky followed with a victory leap, too. And Slugger swam close behind, with Luna keeping a protective eye on the injured dolphin.

Mason hoped the pod would swim close enough to give him Dolphin's Grace. But they didn't. After a few leaps, they dove low again, charting a course through the water that only they remembered.

It's okay, Mason told himself as he quickened his pace. *They'll help me find Asher—and help me and Luna fight any mobs that stand in our way!*

CHAPTER 8

The underwater world had shifted from soft sandstone to sharp rock. Jagged edges reached out toward Mason as he swam by, threatening to catch the straps of his backpack or rip his clothing. *Keep your eyes open,* he told himself. *Watch for danger.*

But swimming was getting tougher now, the water colder and the currents stronger. When Mason fell behind Luna and the pod of dolphins, she circled back, her face awash with worry.

She dug into her backpack and pulled out a potion bottle, but Mason waved his hand. He had already had seconds, taking swigs of water breathing, night vision, and swiftness potions. But being able to see and breathe underwater didn't make his limbs feel any less heavy, and even with potion of swiftness, he couldn't keep up with Luna and the dolphins. They swam too fast!

The dolphins, who had traveled yards ahead, circled back and chattered, as if to say, *C'mon! We have to hurry!*

Mason followed, picturing his brother's face somewhere in the rocky world ahead. Asher needed him. So he kept going.

When the dolphins led Mason and Luna through a narrow crevice in the rock, Mason tried not to panic. *I'll make it through. I'll pretend I'm swimming down the tunnel to Luna's house.*

He took long slow breaths, letting the cool water fill his lungs and then blowing it back out again. *Breathing like a fish,* he thought. *Swimming like a fish. Stroke, flutter kick, stroke, flutter kick, stroke, flutter kick . . .*

As he burst out of the crevice into an open ravine, the light below broke his concentration. It was so bright! *Is it a conduit?* he wondered.

No. The light was orange and flickering. Lava! A checkerboard of magma blocks and black obsidian stretched out at the base of the ravine, spotted with tufts of sea grass.

Mason caught sight of a stream of bubbles floating downward. Down, down, down . . . just like the bubble column he and Asher took every time they returned to their underwater village from the rowboat above.

But this bubble column was wider than theirs—much wider. And *stronger.*

As Mason drifted near the column, the force began to tug at him, dragging him down. But toward what? A sea of lava? Hot magma blocks? A dangerous maze of underwater caves?

No! Mason thrashed his limbs, trying to fight the suction. A memory flickered through his mind of another bubble column, the one that nearly sank Uncle Bart's ship during a storm. Mason remembered the moment the ship had tilted sideways—the horror in Uncle Bart's face as he slid across the deck and right over the rail. *And I never saw him again,* thought Mason.

Fear shot through his body. He swam furiously, trying to fight his way out of the column. But for every upward stroke, the column pulled him down farther. He felt as if his body might split in two.

Help! he wanted to cry. Where was Luna? Where were the dolphins?

He caught sight of Slugger darting past the bubble column—the dolphin that was still recovering from the gash of a drowned's trident.

Mason suddenly remembered the weapon at his side. He couldn't battle a bubble column the way he could battle a drowned, but the enchanted weapon might help him escape.

Mason threw the trident as hard as he could, hoping to break free from the force of the magma block at the base of the bubbles. The trident soared sideways, and Mason felt his body yanked along for the ride.

Thanks to the Riptide enchantment, he flew out of the bubbles and up toward the water's surface. When he got there, Mason nearly cried out with relief.

As the trident slowed, he did too. He reached for his weapon and then searched for Luna. Had she gone down with the column? Was she in trouble?

There she was! She swam toward him, relief etched across her face. Together they veered around the bubble column, searching for the dolphins.

The pod was still circling the bubble column. They darted back toward Mason and Luna, squeaking and squealing, and then forward again, toward the bubbles.

Stay away from the column! Mason wanted to holler. *It's not safe!* So why did the dolphins keep leading them in that direction?

Happy circled back and nudged Luna, as if to say, *Follow me.* But this time, the dolphin carved a wide arc around the bubbles, toward a rocky ledge. When Luna swam toward the ledge, Mason gratefully followed.

A ledge meant that for at least one blissful moment, he wouldn't have to swim. He could rest. He reached out for the ledge and pulled himself upward, stretching out flat on the sheet of rock. He scooched over only far enough for Luna to sit beside him.

Through the water above, Mason could see that the sun was sinking. They'd been swimming all afternoon. But where were they?

He glanced over the ledge to check for the dolphins. The pod swam back and forth just below the rocky outcropping, as if pacing a long narrow room.

They're waiting for us, Mason realized. *But will we ever get to Asher? Are they leading us to him or . . . to somewhere else?*

He felt a stab of panic. What if they'd trusted the dolphins to take them to Asher, but the dolphins were leading them to *different* buried treasure? Away from Asher?

Mason sat up so fast, his backpack caught on a sharp stone. He didn't hear the rip of the fabric, but he felt it. And he watched in frustration as items floated out.

The sea pickle he'd brought to use as a torch toppled off the ledge into the water.

Then the compass—the one that would help Mason and Luna get home if they got separated from the dolphins—spilled out, too. Mason reached for it, but it slipped through his fingers.

Down below, Slugger was already batting at the sea pickle with his snout. He knocked it toward Squeaky, as if starting a game of catch.

Stop! Mason wanted to holler. *Give me back my things!*

But Slugger had gotten a hold of the compass now, too, and was swimming away with it as if it were buried treasure.

Come back! Mason shook his fist. Then he slumped back against the rock, feeling a wave of defeat.

The dolphins hadn't led them to Asher—not yet. And now they were stealing his things. *I've been trying to get the dolphins to trust me,* he realized, *but I'm not even sure I trust them!*

When Luna shot him a questioning glance, he turned away. But as she slipped over the ledge and began swimming with the dolphins, frustration burned in his chest. *Is she going to play with them now, too?* he wondered.

Suddenly, Mason couldn't stand the thought of being underwater for a moment longer. He pushed away from the ledge and swam up instead of down.

As his head burst out of the water, he took a gulp of cool air. He glanced at the watery world around him, then froze.

A beach spread out before him, extending for miles toward a snow-capped mountain range. But this was like no beach Mason had seen before.

Instead of sand, the shoreline was bathed in rock and gravel. A battered rowboat rested on the rocks, as if it had crashed against them and been abandoned. Just beyond the shore, stone slopes stretched upward toward the majestic mountains and the blue sky above.

Something nudged Mason from below—a gentle bump to his rear that sent him forward toward the shore. A dolphin's fin broke the water's surface. Then Luna's dark head popped out of the waves. She sucked in her breath, catching sight of the mountains. "Where are we?" she asked, wiping her eyes.

"I don't know," Mason whispered.

But maybe Asher is here, too, he thought suddenly. And he began to swim.

CHAPTER 9

As Mason pulled himself out of the water onto a rock, he felt as if his body weighed a thousand pounds.

The first thing he did was pick his way across the rocks toward the rowboat. Had Asher been in the boat? Mason searched for clues, but the hull was empty. As he slid the paddle sideways, a silverfish scuttled out and disappeared over the boat's edge. Mason grimaced and dropped the paddle back down.

Then he glanced up at the steep shoreline. *If Asher is here, he must have made his way up.* Mason began to climb, hand over hand. But his foot slipped on the wet rocks, tugging him downward again.

Was Luna following? He turned to find her.

Luna sat on a rock below, shading her eyes against the setting sun. "Where are the dolphins?" she asked.

Mason shrugged. "They can't follow us here." For just a moment, he wondered if he and Luna were taking the right path. The dolphins couldn't have led

Asher to buried treasure on this rocky shoreline, could they? He hesitated.

"There—I see them!" Luna pointed at the trio of fins flitting through the waves just off shore.

A turquoise head poked out of the water, and Squeaky chattered a greeting. Or was it a goodbye?

Then something else sailed out of the water. It arced through the air and landed on the rocks with a clatter.

"What is it?" Luna asked, picking her away across the rocks toward the object.

Mason already knew what she would find. "My compass!" he cried. "Slugger gave it back." *Maybe because he knows we'll need it,* he thought to himself. Maybe it was a sign—a sign that they were on the right path toward finding Asher.

As soon as Luna retrieved the compass, Mason began climbing again. Asher was close by—he could feel it! And that gave him the energy to pull with his arms and push off with his legs, to climb the wall that seemed to go straight up. Up, up, up . . .

He reached the top just as the sun sank below the horizon. A breeze ruffled his hair as he lifted his head over the rocky edge. What would he find? Another mountain to climb?

Mason was relieved to see flat shoreline extending into the shadows ahead—a field of gray gravel and rock. With one last heave, he pulled himself up and then rolled away from the edge.

"Can I get a hand?" Luna called from below.

Mason sighed and sat up, leaning down to help his friend. He gripped her hand and pulled until she joined him on the gravel ledge. She held her stomach, trying to catch her breath.

"Do you think Asher made that climb alone?" she asked, voicing what Mason had been thinking.

"If he knew there was buried treasure at the top, he'd scale that wall in a flash," Mason said.

Luna grinned. "True." She studied the mountains. "But where'd he go next?"

Mason cupped his mouth and hollered. "Asher!" His brother's name bounced off the snow-capped mountaintops and circled right back. *Ash-er! Ash-er! Ash-er!*

A sudden gust of wind blew across the gravel beach, spraying tiny stones. Then something else whizzed overhead.

Mason ducked and sucked in his breath. "Was that a phantom?" he whispered, remembering the winged beasts that had tormented him when he and Asher had been shipwrecked on the beach.

Luna shook her head so hard, her wet ponytail flung sideways. "Not phantoms," she cried. "Skeletons!"

Skeletons. The word sounded foreign to Mason. It had been so long since he'd battled mobs on land, mobs other than drowned or guardians. He grabbed his trident, not sure he even knew what to do with it. What good was the Riptide enchantment against skeletons?

As a spray of arrows flew overhead, Luna grabbed

his arm. "Let's get back down, behind the ledge!" she urged.

Mason scrambled to follow her, so fast that his foot slipped. He tumbled over the ledge, his backpack strap catching on a jagged point. He hung there for just a moment—until his instincts kicked in, and he grasped the rocks with both hands.

But grabbing the rocks meant letting go of the trident. It fell to the rocks below with a clatter.

As the sound rang out, Mason locked eyes with Luna. Fear flickered across her face, then determination. She handed him her trident. "Use this," she said. "I have potions."

Luna's trident felt heavy and slippery in Mason's sweaty hand. He struggled to hold it while also gripping the rock.

"Are they coming?" Luna called over her shoulder as she dug into her backpack.

Mason swallowed hard and willed himself to extend his neck, just above the highest rock. Yes—the skeletons were definitely coming. Except they *weren't* skeletons.

"Spider jockeys!" Mason cried, unable to tear his eyes away from the spiders crossing the gravel beach. Three of them crawled across the stones, their red eyes glowing in the night. Three furry-legged beasts, with three skeleton riders. And all three jockeys had their bows drawn.

Thwack, thwack! Two more arrows whizzed over Mason's head, so close that one tickled his hair.

"Throw the trident!" said Luna.

Mason tried. He gripped it tightly and swung his arm back, hoping to get some momentum. But how could he, when he was clinging to the rocks for safety? The trident sailed only a few yards before nose-diving into the ground.

Mason's stomach nose-dived, too, until he saw the trident pull itself free and sail back to him—right into his palm. The Loyalty enchantment! *I have another chance,* he realized. *As many as I need.*

So he threw again. This time, the trident struck a spider in the chest. It screeched with rage, shrugged free of the weapon, and charged forward, its eyes blazing red.

The other spider jockey overtook the first. They were so close now!

Thwack!

Mason dodged an arrow but held out his hand, desperate for the trident to return.

It did, just in time. He threw it again and heard the satisfying grunt of a skeleton. He'd hit a jockey, knocking it right off the spider. But there were two more coming, just a stone's throw away.

Or a *potion's* throw. Luna readied her bottle and threw. The glass shattered against the rocks.

Mason couldn't see the bubbles drifting upward, but he knew it was a lingering potion—a splash potion that would create a toxic cloud, a barrier of bubbles between them and the spider jockeys. And if those hostile mobs dared to pass through it . . .

Another spider screeched, and a skeleton hit the ground with a jangle of bones. Mason dared a peek over the rocks and saw only one jockey remained. The spider had come to a stop just beyond the cloud of bubbles. Only its eyes shone through—red beams that locked in on Mason.

He sucked in his breath and threw the trident with every ounce of strength he could muster.

The weapon hit its mark. The spider squealed and scuttled backward. *Yes!* Mason pumped his fist and caught the trident that came sailing back. But something else came, too.

Thwack!

As another arrow sailed overhead, a sickening realization washed over Mason.

The last spider was dead, but the skeleton was *not*. And it was coming for them.

CHAPTER 10

Mason heard the tinkle of bones just beyond the ridge of rock. As he glanced up, he saw the tip of an arrow. The skeleton stood just above the ledge, its bow pointing down.

Mason stared into the gaping eye sockets of the undead mob—and froze.

He squeezed his eyes shut and had one last thought: *Please let Asher be okay.* Then he heard the arrow whizzing through the air.

And a grunt.

Mason's eyes flung open just as the skeleton toppled off the ledge, down to the rocky shore below. He whirled around to see Luna's satisfied smile. She held a pickaxe—a tiny weapon. But it had been enough to knock the spider off its bony feet.

Luna blew out her breath. "They're gone," she said, wiping the sweat off her forehead. "Now let's find a safe place to wait out the night, before more mobs show up."

As Mason followed her back up over the rocks, he felt light and giddy with relief. *But more mobs could spawn at any second,* he reminded himself. He kept a tight hold on Luna's trident while she pulled flint and steel out of her pack. In seconds, she had lit a torch.

They began to jog across the gravel beach, searching for shelter. But all Mason could see was the bobbing pool of light on the ground ahead of them. The mountains in the distance were cloaked in black.

He studied that gravel, wondering if it would be soft enough to tunnel into. *Maybe we can dig out an underground cave to sleep in,* he thought. *Maybe we can . . .*

Something caught his eye on the ground, and he came to a sudden stop. Were those footprints? He squatted and studied the tread of each oblong print. Then his chest flooded with relief. "They're Asher's sneakers!" he cried. "This is his trail!"

Luna crouched beside the prints. "Yes, that must be him!"

Mason's heart raced as he ran along the path his brother had left. Judging by the zig-zagging trail, Mason could tell Asher hadn't known which way to go. The dolphins had led him to this shoreline, but he'd been on his own after that.

After a few yards, Asher's trail faded . . . and disappeared. "What happened?" Mason cried out, dropping to his knees.

Luna held the torch high, but even in the light, they couldn't find Asher's next step. The path was smeared—the gravel scattered in all directions—just beside a triangular rock.

Mason searched the darkness. "Asher!" he called. But only the echo of his own voice bounced back.

He shivered as he pushed himself up, leaning on the rock for support. That's when he saw it—the glint of something silver. "Shine the light!" he said to Luna, waving her toward the rock.

As soon as the torch lit the ground, Mason's heart sank. A pickaxe was resting on the ground just beside the rock. *Asher's* pickaxe—Mason could tell by the slight chip in the blade.

His brother would never leave his axe behind. It was the only way to mine for treasure. It was his only weapon!

Mason grabbed the axe and spun in a circle. "Asher!" he cried again. "Where are you?"

The answer came so suddenly, Mason feared he'd imagined it. "Here!" His brother's voice sounded muffled.

"Where?"

"Here!"

This time, it sounded as if Asher were right beside them. But where? Mason studied the shadows. As he stepped around the triangular rock, he slipped. His foot gave way, and suddenly he was sinking downward into the gravel.

He grasped for the rock and caught it with his fingertips. "Luna, help!" he cried.

She was already there, tugging his arm. She pulled

him backward toward more solid ground. As Mason fell onto his rear, he heard Asher cry out again. "Stop! Don't move!"

Was the voice coming from the ground below? Had Asher been caught in the rockslide, too? And . . . fallen?

Mason carefully brushed the gravel off his scraped-up shins and rolled onto his knees. "Asher, are you down there? Are you trapped?"

A moment of silence passed. Then Asher's strained voice filtered up through the rocky ground. "Yes."

Mason's stomach clenched. He watched as Luna crawled closer to the sunken hole and brushed it carefully with her hand. More rocks fell, as if pouring into a bucket.

"Stop!" Asher cried again. "You're making it worse!"

She quickly pulled her hand back. "What's down there?" she asked. "An abandoned mineshaft? A sea cave?"

"I don't know," came Asher's response. "A cave, I guess. It's half full of water."

Mason sucked in his breath. "How do we get to him?" he whispered to Luna, pushing himself to his feet. "Can we lower a rope or something?"

Luna stared back at her pack. "I didn't bring one. Did you?"

He shook his head and began to pace. "I told him not to leave the safety of the conduit," he muttered. "But all he could think about was buried treasure. And look where it got him!"

Luna stared at the ground. "No wonder the

dolphins came for us," she said. "They must have known he was trapped. But . . . what happened to the other dolphins?" She leaned toward the ground. "Asher, are Simon and Hungry with you?"

"Yes!"

Mason felt a ripple of relief. Asher wasn't alone. The dolphins were with him. But . . . how could they be? "Simon and Hungry can't leave the water," he said, thinking out loud. "How did they get into the cave, Asher?"

After a pause, Asher responded. "I don't know! They found me here after I fell. But then there was another rockslide and . . . now they're trapped, too."

Luna chewed her lip. "There must be another way into the cave," she said to Mason. "How do we find it?"

The answer struck Mason like a lightning bolt. "The bubble column!" he cried. "The dolphins kept swimming toward it, as if leading us down it. Remember?"

Luna nodded slowly.

"So maybe there's an entrance to the flooded cave at the base of the ravine," he said. He whirled around so fast, he nearly launched forward into the sinkhole again. "Asher, we're coming," he told his brother. "Don't worry. We're going to find you."

Luna was on her feet now, too, pulling potions from her pack. "If we're going down the bubble column, we have to be ready," she said.

"I know," Mason said. "Let's do it!"

He swallowed the liquid so fast, he almost choked.

Then he slid Asher's pickaxe into his backpack and began to run toward the rocky shore.

*   *   *

Mason didn't climb back into the water—he leaped. Could he remember the way back to the bubble column? He wasn't sure. But the potion of night vision was kicking in now. *I just have to look for the magma blocks below,* he reminded himself. *They'll glow and light my way.*

Luna glided past, and then someone else—or something else—did, too. A dolphin!

Mason recognized Happy, who looked especially happy now that Mason and Luna were back in the water. He heard Squeaky chattering nearby, and then Slugger zoomed by, taking the lead.

Mason didn't have to search for magma blocks— the dolphins led him straight to the bubble column. Instantly, he felt the tug of the water on his body. And this time, he let it take him.

As he zoomed downward, he imagined he was in the bubble column, heading toward home. But home looked *nothing* like this. Jagged rock walls stretched upward in all directions. Mason felt trapped, like a zombie in a pit. He fought the panic rising in his chest. *Asher is down here,* he reminded himself. *We have to find Asher.* He took a long, steadying breath of cool water.

As the ocean floor rose to greet him, Mason leaped out of the column, swimming sideways to avoid stepping on the hot magma blocks. He glanced back to be sure Luna was following.

She burst out of the bubble column behind him and swam through a clump of sea grass. Then the dolphins were there too, diving down from somewhere up above. As soon as they hit bottom, the dolphins were off, darting along the base of a rock wall.

Mason pushed off from the ocean floor and swam, paddling fiercely through the water. The dolphins knew where Asher was—he could feel it! And they'd reach him soon, very soon.

The dolphins suddenly reversed direction, so quickly that Mason had to paddle backward to avoid running into the gravel wall ahead. Squeaky began squealing, swimming back and forth along the wall. Slugger nosed at a hunk of rock, as if trying to burrow through.

And then Mason knew.

The wall of gravel must have tumbled down from the beach above. That gravel wall was the only thing separating the dolphins from the rest of their pod.

Simon and Hungry were trapped behind that wall of rock.

And Asher was, too.

CHAPTER 11

Mason pulled Asher's pickaxe from his backpack and began to swing. He whacked at the
gravel over and over. Luna was mining, too,
tunneling her way through the gravel wall.

Each swing of the axe sent ripples through the
water. Mason could barely see the gravel in front of
him. Behind, Squeaky chattered nervously, as if to say,
Hurry!

I'm trying! Mason couldn't swing any faster, any
harder. Finally, his axe broke through. As rock crum-
bled away, a small hole formed.

Mason used his hands to clear the opening. Then
he half pushed, half pulled himself through. He opened
his eyes and was surprised to see light shining through
the water above. He swam upward until his head broke
free.

He was inside a large sea cave, mostly filled with
water. A pile of rock and gravel rose out of the water.

Above that, a trickle of moonlight shone through a small slit in the roof of the cave.

Thanks to potion of night vision, Mason could make out a figure crouched on the rocks. "Asher?" Mason rubbed his eyes.

"It's me!" Asher responded.

Relief tingled from Mason's head to his toes. He swam toward the rocks, and Asher helped him crawl up and out of the murky water.

Asher's shirt was torn and dirty. His helmet sat askew, his red hair sticking out from it in every direction. And his eyes drooped, as if he'd been awake for days. But he was alive. Mason nearly hugged him.

"How did you get in?" asked Asher.

"We tunneled our way through the gravel," Mason said. He pointed down at the water just as Luna's head broke free.

"Asher!" she cried, nearly choking on his name.

Then a dolphin leaped out of the water beside her. And another. While Squeaky chattered and chirped, Slugger and Happy darted this way and that, as if searching for their pod mates.

"The other dolphins!" Luna said as she climbed out of the water. "Where are Simon and Hungry?"

Asher pointed to the other side of the rock. "There," he said. "They're trapped!"

Mason followed Asher's gaze toward the shallow pool of water, cut off from the rest of the water by the gravel that had fallen from above. Two fins swam back and forth.

Luna glanced around the cave. "I think the water's rising," she said. "It's probably gushing in through the tunnel we made. When it gets high enough, it'll cover the rock. Then Simon and Hungry will be able to swim free!"

"Yes!" Asher said. "And we will, too—*finally*." He clutched his stomach. "Did you bring food? I haven't eaten in ages."

Luna unzipped her backpack and pulled out a bag of dried kelp. Asher gobbled down the salty flakes. He dug greedily into the bag of cooked cod that Luna offered him, too.

A few months ago, he wouldn't touch the stuff, Mason remembered. Asher still wouldn't eat salmon, but he'd learned to like cod.

"Save some for the rest of us!" Luna scolded. But when Asher glanced at her with hungry eyes, she waved her hand. "Oh, go ahead. You've had a rough day."

Together, they sat on the rock and waited. The water rose, slowly but steadily. Then a noise sounded overhead.

Mason ducked. "What was that?" he cried. "A bat?"

Asher nodded. "They live here. Don't worry, they won't bite. I mean, I don't *think* they will . . ." He chewed his lip.

Luna waved her hand. "Bats are harmless."

But up above, something else was spawning. Mason could almost feel it—the ground shaking with footsteps. Then he heard the groan. "Zombies?" he whispered.

Something grunted in response.

Luna quickly lit a torch and waved it around the cave, searching. "They're not in here," she said. "They must be above us."

Sure enough, footsteps thundered overhead. Mason sucked in his breath. "It sounds like there are a lot of them," he said.

Stones trickled down through the slit in the roof, and then a steady stream began to splash into the water below.

"Rockslide!" cried Asher. He dove sideways into the shallow pool of water.

Mason dove the other way, accidentally taking Luna with him. He swam lower and lower, feeling the water churn overhead with every dropping stone. Dark shapes darted past—dolphins, who seemed just as anxious as he was.

Finally, the rockslide slowed. Mason waited, treading water, until the water was calm. Then he slowly and carefully made his way back up toward the light.

When he broke free of the water, his heart sank. A mound of gravel now split the cave in two, and Asher was nowhere in sight.

"Asher!" As Mason called out, a few more stones slid downward. "Asher," he said more quietly. "Are you okay?"

After a long, terrifying moment, he heard a response. "I'm here!" Asher sounded so far away.

Luna sprang out of the water beside Mason. "Oh, no," she whispered. "We have to dig him out!"

"Wait!" Mason held up his hand, treading water with the other. "If we try to mine through this, we'll just bring down more rocks. And Asher might get—" He couldn't finish the sentence.

He glanced upward, where a smidge of light still shone through the roof of the cave. "We should climb up and out," he said. "Maybe Asher can do the same from the other side!"

"No!" Asher's voice sounded louder now—and very firm. "I'm not leaving my dolphins."

"But . . ." Mason glanced at Luna, who shrugged. She wouldn't leave the dolphins behind either—Mason was sure of that. Since Luna and Asher had been granted Dolphin's Grace, it was as if they had become members of the pod.

Mason sighed. "Then we'll have to find another way." He began to swim laps, thinking.

We can't go up because dolphins can't climb. We can't go through the gravel wall, because more rocks will fall. But maybe . . .

He popped out of the water beside Luna. "Can we tunnel *around* the gravel?" he asked. He pointed toward the wall of the cave.

Luna shrugged. "It's worth a shot." She pulled the pickaxe from her backpack, and Mason slid Asher's axe from his own.

Together, they dove just below the water's surface and began to mine—more carefully this time, so as not to disturb the rocks. Slugger helped, nosing the mined blocks away with his snout.

They tunneled three blocks into the wall, and veered left. But how *far* left should they tunnel? Mason wasn't sure. If they mined too far, they'd miss Asher completely. *But if we don't go far enough, we'll tunnel our way right into the gravel wall—and cause another rockslide!* Mason swallowed hard and kept mining.

Finally, he stopped swinging and gazed left. Something in his gut told him this was far enough. He hoped his gut was right.

He glanced at Luna, who nodded. He swung his axe.

Clink, clink! One block popped out.

Clink, clink, clink! Luna tunneled through another.

Mason held his breath as he whacked the last block. As it dislodged from the wall, he could see straight through to the watery cavern on the other side. A freckled face appeared in the mined hole—and grinned.

Yes!

Mason helped his brother swim into the tunnel. But would the dolphins follow? He held his breath and waited.

Hungry nosed at the hole with his long snout, but quickly darted away. *Simon has to lead him,* Mason realized. *C'mon, Simon!*

But the lead dolphin wouldn't swim through. He swam past, left and right, his scarred side appearing for just a moment before disappearing again.

Mason glanced at his brother, who hovered near the hole. His mouth was set in a grim line. The glow of his enchanted helmet had begun to dim. Would he run out of oxygen soon?

I have to get him out of here! thought Mason. But another realization followed close behind. *We have to get the dolphins to follow us. Because if they won't go . . .*

. . . Asher won't either.

CHAPTER 12

Asher left his dolphins only long enough to drink Luna's potions of water breathing and night vision.

"How are we going to get them out?" he asked, wiping a dribble of potion off his chin.

"I don't know," said Mason. But as he watched Luna zip up her pack, a torch flickered to life in his mind, as if powered by redstone. "The cod!" he said, pointing at Luna's pack. "Could we use it to lure Simon and Hungry out of the hole?"

Luna pursed her lips and glanced at Asher, whose face fell. "I sort of ate it all," he confessed.

"Oh." Mason's stomach sank.

"I didn't know the dolphins would need it!" Asher said. "But now . . . they do. I'm sorry." He sighed. Then he slipped back into the water and started swimming toward the tunnel in the wall.

"Asher, wait!" Mason called, hoping to stall his

brother. Could he convince him to leave the dolphins behind?

Can I even leave them behind? Mason wondered. He slowly nodded. If it meant saving his brother, he could—and he would. So he asked Asher the one thing that could take his brother's mind off of Simon and Hungry, at least for a moment. "Did you find the buried treasure?"

Asher stopped swimming and started treading water. His face spread into a smile. "Yeah," he said. "I found it—just before the rockslide took me down. The treasure chest fell into the cave with me. It's back there, on the other side of the gravel." He pointed, and his eyes lit up. He stuck his fist in the air. "That's it!"

He took off swimming so fast, Mason sucked in his breath. "What happened?" he asked Luna. "What did I say?"

She shrugged and dove into the water, following Asher. So Mason did, too.

Through the dark tunnel they swam, one by one, until they'd reached the pool of water on the other end. Mason searched the shallow pool for Asher, and saw his legs dangling in the water from the rocks up above. Mason quickly climbed out and found his brother sitting beside a treasure chest. The wooden chest was splintered and swollen with water.

When Asher cracked opened the lid, Mason scooted over to see what was inside. His brother pulled out a red and white block of TNT and set it on a flat rock.

"What—?" Mason started to ask. Was Asher going

to blow his way out of the cave? That would never work! It would only cause an even bigger and more dangerous landslide.

But Asher had moved on, digging deeper into the chest. He scooped out a few turquoise prismarine crystals, which made Mason smile. "Just what you were hoping for," he joked. "Now you can help me make a sea lantern and finish the conduit!"

The conduit. The underwater village and their home felt so far away. *It's too soon to think about that,* thought Mason, shaking his head. *We have a long way to go before we get there.*

As Asher tucked the crystals into his pocket, Mason stared back into the treasure chest. Something glittered from the bottom. A diamond!

"Asher, you found real treasure!" Luna said. She had climbed onto the rocks and now stood over the chest, water dripping from her hair and clothes onto the treasures below.

Asher barely seemed to notice her. He pushed the diamond aside as if it were a lump of coal, and reached for something beneath it.

The smell hit Mason first—the scent of the fishiest fish. *Salmon.* Asher lifted a hunk of cooked salmon with his fingertips, as if the fish was the most disgusting thing he'd ever touched. He scrunched up his nose. But his eyes lit up as he asked, "Will the dolphins eat this? Could we use it to lure them into the tunnel?"

As if in response, Hungry leaped out of the water,

inches away from the salmon. Asher pulled it back toward his chest.

"I think you just got your answer!" Mason said, laughing. "But break it into little pieces. We're going to have to make it last."

Asher tore the hunk of fish into four or five pieces. Then he slipped back into the water, leaving the treasure chest on the rocks with the lid wide open.

Mason watched, holding his breath. If Asher's plan worked, they could be out of the cave in no time, heading back toward safety. Back toward *home*.

Asher swam a couple of feet into the tunnel. Then he spun around and held out the hunk of salmon, using it like a lure. When Hungry darted toward it, Asher turned and swam away. Would Hungry follow?

Go after it! Mason wanted to shout.

Hungry didn't. He darted away from the tunnel entrance and swam back and forth, squeaking with frustration. The dolphin wanted that fish—he really did.

So why won't he go after it? Mason wondered.

Asher appeared at the tunnel entrance again, dangling the fish like a prize. This time, Hungry didn't go for the treat at all. But someone else did.

Simon, the fearless leader, swam toward Asher, nosing the fish with his snout. Asher let him eat it and instantly held out another hunk. But before Simon could eat it, Asher turned and led the dolphin down the tunnel.

Mason watched, barely moving a muscle, as Hungry swam slowly after Simon. The dolphin hesitated at the tunnel entrance for just a moment before darting inside and disappearing.

Yes! Mason's heart leaped in his chest.

Luna spun around and gave him a thumbs-up. "Our turn to go," she said, diving into the water.

Mason slid off the rocks behind her and swam toward the hole. He followed the murky shapes ahead, knowing Asher was leading the dolphins to safety. When he heard the chatter on the other end of the tunnel, he knew they'd been reunited with the rest of their pod. At last!

When Mason broke free of the tunnel, he swam upward, hoping for a breath of fresh air. He could still see the moonlight above. But was it glowing *green*?

He followed Luna's kicking feet and finally reached the surface. But as soon as his head popped out of the water, he shaded his eyes against the bright green glow. It bounced off the cave walls. Where was it coming from?

Then he saw.

Something had spawned in the cavern while they were on the other side.

Something wet. Something squishy.

Slime!

CHAPTER 13

Mason dove quickly underwater, inhaling water instead of air. He drew his trident carefully, trying not to hit the dolphins—or Luna or Asher—as he got ready to fight the slime.

But the water around him had grown so dim. *My potion of night vision is wearing off!* he realized.

He squinted, trying to make out the shapes in the murky water. A dolphin darted past, and was that a slime floating above? Mason gripped his trident, preparing to swing. But what if he hit another dolphin? He couldn't chance it!

Instead, he swam to the wall of the cave and then upward. He broke free of the water, and suddenly realized just how high the water had risen. Only a few feet remained between Mason and the top of the cave—and that space was *filled* with floating mobs. Squishy, sloppy slimes.

Squish, splash, squish, splash, squish . . . One bounced between the ceiling and the water, bobbling along the water's surface toward Mason. He swung his arm backward, preparing to throw his trident.

Whack! Pain shot through his arm and shoulder as his trident struck the wall of the cave. He tried to swing again, but his arm had gone numb.

Squish, splash, squish, splash, squish . . . splat!

Mason shrank backward just as the slime burst into pieces. Then something whizzed through the air— Luna's trident returning to her hand. *She* had struck the slime just in time.

Now mini slimes filled the water. A dolphin surfaced, nudging a slime with its snout. Slugger!

Mason lunged for the dolphin's fin, hoping to pull him away. *It's not a toy!* he wanted to cry. *The slime will hurt you!*

And it did. With a squeal, Slugger retreated from the mini slime and dove down.

But that single squeal alerted the other dolphins. Mason felt them churning through the water below, ready to battle the slimes. But he couldn't see them. He couldn't see *anything*.

And if the water kept rising, he wouldn't be able to breathe.

I need Luna's potions! he realized, searching for her. But there were too many bodies in the shadows. A battle was raging, and all Mason could do was try to stay calm and *think*.

He treaded water, trying to stay afloat. *Thud!* His forehead suddenly hit the ceiling. The water had risen so high! The cave was almost fully flooded now. Mason tilted his chin upward and sucked in air.

When something thrashed beside him, Mason's hand tightened on his trident. Then he heard Asher's voice.

"The dolphins!" Asher said, coughing and sputtering water. "They won't be able to breathe!"

Huh? Mason couldn't respond—he was too busy taking breaths of his own. Then he remembered. The dolphins would need to surface soon, too. *They need water to survive, but they also need air,* Luna had told them.

For just a moment, he wanted to scold Asher. *What about us?* Mason wanted to say. *How can you worry about the dolphins when we're fighting for our own lives?*

But he didn't. As another dolphin squealed in pain or anger, and another slime burst into pieces, Mason grabbed his brother's arm. "We have to get out of here," he said. "We'll swim out the way we came in. Follow me!"

He took one more breath of air—he was going to need it. Then he dove down, as low as he could go. He hoped Asher would follow, and that Luna and the dolphins would, too.

We're in this together, Mason thought. *All of us.*

As he swam past Luna, he grabbed her backpack to get her attention. She swung around so furiously, he feared she'd hit him with her trident. Then he waved his arm. *Follow me. Let's go!*

Down, down, down he swam, feeling his way rather than seeing it. The opening they'd made in the gravel *had* to be here somewhere. And it would lead them out—out to the base of the ravine, where they could swim free.

His hands sorted through sharp stones, searching for the opening. Finally they broke through. He wiggled his fingers in the water beyond. *Yes!*

But just as he began to swim through, something knocked him backward. A small slime slid past, leaving a slippery trail on Mason's arm. Then the opening was gone—plugged by a squishy, bloated green block.

No! Mason thought, punching the slime. It punched back. Instantly, Mason sank, feeling too weak to swim or stand.

His lungs burned, begging for air. But Luna and her potions were high above. She was battling for her own life. And Asher? Had he followed? Mason felt too weak to turn. Too weak to even look.

So this is how it's going to end, he thought as his body slumped against a bed of gravel. *Please just let Asher make it out. Please!*

Suddenly, a thrust from behind knocked Mason forward, toward the opening in the gravel. He flung his arms out, trying to brace himself so he wouldn't hit the slime.

But the slime was gone—broken into a thousand mini pieces. Slime balls floated past, too small now to do damage. Too small to block Mason's path to freedom.

But I'm too weak to swim, he realized. *I can't swim through!*

Another nudge from behind sent him halfway through the hole. He could see the magma blocks on the other side—the fiery patch of lava and obsidian. It gave him the strength to pull himself forward.

As he broke free to the other side, he glanced up at the sky, searching for the moon. But it was the morning sun that filtered through the water above. *Way* too high above. *I'll never make it to the water's surface!* Mason thought with a stab of fear.

He couldn't hold his breath any longer—he knew he couldn't. But just as he opened his mouth, ready to let the water in, he was lifted from the ocean floor and carried forward.

He glanced down and saw a square gray snout beneath him. *Slugger.* That was Mason's last thought before the dolphin tossed him forward into a spray of bubbles.

*   *   *

Mason opened his eyes. Something was shaking him—hard. Luna's worried face appeared inches from his own, bubbles floating down all around her. He opened his mouth to speak, but he couldn't. He was still underwater.

But I can breathe! he realized. Had Luna slipped him some potion?

No. As a dolphin circled past, Mason saw where he was: in the middle of the bubble column, where he could fill his lungs with pure, sweet air.

The magma block below tugged him down, but Luna held him up, keeping him from burning himself on the fiery rocks.

Good old Luna, he thought with a smile. Then he thought of someone else. "Asher!" His brother's name came out in a flurry of bubbles.

Luna smiled. She gave Mason a thumbs-up and pointed toward Asher, who was chasing a dolphin's tail. His brother was *surrounded* by dolphins, and grinning ear to ear.

We made it out, Mason thought. *All of us.* That realization gave him the strength to swim out of the bubble column. He pointed up, toward the water's surface.

Luna nodded. She darted back through the bubble column, as if to get one last breath of air. Then she waved at Asher to do the same.

Mason watched in wonder as the dolphins followed Asher in, swimming through the bubbles as if filling their own lungs too. Asher led them in and out as confidently as Simon himself. Then they started streaming upward, like a dolphin parade, soaring up toward the morning sky.

Mason's legs felt strong, propelling him forward with each kick. But his right arm and shoulder still tingled from his run-in with the cave wall. He wished he could grab hold of a dolphin's tail and go along for the ride.

Maybe someday, he thought. *Maybe someday they'll trust me enough to let me swim with them, like Asher does. But for now, we just have to get home.*

When his head finally popped out of the water, he closed his eyes and turned his face toward the sun. The warmth felt so good!

Then he squinted to see the others. Simon and Happy were putting on a show, leaping high out of the water. And Asher?

There he was, straightening out his helmet. He waved at Mason. "C'mon!" he called.

As Mason took a stroke toward his brother, a jolt of pain ran down his right arm. He flipped onto his back to rest.

"What's wrong?" asked Asher, swimming up beside him.

"I hurt my shoulder," said Mason, wincing. "I'm not going to be able to swim very far like this."

"Luna has potion of healing," Asher said brightly. "She'll fix you up—you'll see."

But as Mason rolled onto his side, he caught sight of Luna staring off at the horizon. At what?

Then he saw it—Luna's orange backpack! It had caught a wave and was drifting out to sea, bobbing further away with each passing second.

That backpack holds her healing potion, Mason realized, with another stab of pain. *That backpack holds ALL her potions!*

CHAPTER 14

"**W**hy isn't she swimming after it?" Asher asked. "Go, Luna! Go get your backpack!" He slapped his hand against the water, urging her on.

But Luna had stopped swimming. Her dark head bobbed in the waves as she stared after the lost pack, which sank out of view.

"She must be too tired," Mason said, feeling the weight of his own weary body pulling him down.

When Asher took off swimming after Luna, Mason tried to follow. He rolled onto his left side and side-stroked, letting his right arm rest. But he couldn't see above the rolling waves. *Am I swimming in circles?* he wondered.

Then he heard voices. Asher and Luna were close by.

"We can't get home without the potions," said Luna. Her voice sounded thin and tight, as if she were at her breaking point.

"Maybe the dolphins will help us," said Asher.

In the silence that followed, Mason flipped onto his stomach and took a couple of painful strokes to reach his brother.

Then Luna said four words that cut right through the waves. "The dolphins are *gone*."

Mason wiped his eyes and followed her gaze. A few fins zig-zagged in the distance, heading out to sea.

"How could they leave us?" Asher asked in a tiny voice.

Mason took a deep breath. "We'll be okay," he told his brother. "The dolphins did what you wanted them to do—they led you to treasure, right?"

Asher shook his wet head. "But I didn't even take all the treasure! I was too busy trying to save the dolphins!" He slapped at the water again.

He's not mad about the treasure, Mason thought. *Not really.* For once, Asher seemed to have found something he cared about *more* than diamonds and emeralds. He'd found some friends—but now he'd lost them.

"C'mon," Mason said gently. "Let's get back to shore. We have to rest."

"And we have to make a plan," Luna added. "A plan for how in the Overworld we're going to get home."

Her words gave Mason a chill. Or maybe it was the cool water and the wet clothes he'd been wearing for what felt like days. The rocky shore, lit by the morning sun, suddenly looked inviting.

"Let's go," he said, taking the lead.

With each stroke toward shore, he tried to ignore the pain in his shoulder. But his strokes grew weaker and weaker. Finally, he stopped swimming altogether, trying to catch his breath.

As Luna and Asher passed him by, Mason studied the shoreline. He thought back to the steep climb up the rocky wall. *Will I be able to scale the wall again today? With only one good arm?*

He searched the coast for another path up. Then he saw it—the most beautiful sight he'd seen in days. The weathered old rowboat sat perched on the jagged rocks.

We can *get home!* Mason thought with a jolt of hope. *We have a boat!*

He began swimming again, faster and faster, toward shore.

* * *

The boat had seen better days. The oak hull had faded from brown to gray, and only one paddle remained. Mason grimaced, remembering the silverfish that had scuttled out from underneath it just yesterday. He slid the paddle sideways to make sure no other critters remained.

"Will it float?" Asher asked, kicking the boat with the toe of his sneaker.

"Let's hope so," Luna said. She refastened her wet ponytail. "C'mon."

They loaded in their things, or at least what was left of them: their tridents, pickaxes, and Mason's backpack. As he tossed the pack onto the seat of the boat, he remembered something. "My compass!" He pulled the tool out and studied it. "Slugger brought this back to me when I thought I'd lost it. Maybe he knew we'd have to get home on our own."

Mason had hoped the words would make Asher smile—would remind him that the dolphins were looking out for their human friends, even if they weren't going to stay with them forever.

But Asher just shrugged and leaned toward the boat. "Help me push this old thing," he said.

Together, they slowly slid the boat off the sharp rocks. "Careful!" Mason said. "We don't want to damage the bottom of the boat." *If it's not damaged already.* He kept that last thought to himself.

Once the boat was bobbing in the shallow water, Mason held up the compass. Luna was already rowing, heading away from the rocks the way they had come. She took strong strokes, as if she couldn't wait to get away from the stony shore. Away from the slimes they had battled underground. Away from rockslides and spider jockeys and underground ravines.

I can't either, Mason thought. But as he hollered directions—"Head southwest! No, that's east, Asher. Paddle on the other side!"—he noticed the water puddling at his feet.

Please let that be trickling off Asher's oar, he thought, swallowing hard. He quickly glanced over his shoulder, wondering if there was time to go back to dry land.

Nope. The stony store was just a slim ridge of rock in the distance. *We could never swim back that far. At least, I couldn't . . .* Mason squeezed his injured shoulder.

As the water reached his ankles, his mind scrambled, trying to come up with a solution. Should he tell Luna? Could he alert her to the rising water without freaking out his little brother?

In the split second that passed, Mason got his answer.

"Yikes!" Asher squealed, staring down at his feet.

Too late.

"The boat's gonna sink!" Asher cried. "What do we do?"

Luna whirled around. She stared at Mason with worried eyes.

Mason gave a weak shrug. "I don't know," he said. "I think . . . we're going to have to swim."

CHAPTER 15

Luna began paddling backward. "We can't swim all the way back to shore! We have to paddle as far as we can," she said.

"I can't even see shore!" Asher said. "We're in the middle of nowhere."

"Just paddle!" Luna barked.

When Asher fell back limply against the seat, Mason grabbed his oar and began shoving water away, moving the boat backward. Every stroke tore at his shoulder, but he kept going. What else could he do?

The water rose to their knees. The boat sat so low now, it felt as if it weighed a thousand pounds. Mason struggled to move the oar through the waves, and then finally sat back.

"I . . . can't," he said. "I have to rest my arm."

Luna started to protest, but as the boat tipped side to side, water sloshed over its rim. "Then we'll have to swim," she whispered. "Without potions."

In the silence that followed, water drip, drip, dripped over the side. Fear trickled down Mason's spine, too. How could he protect Asher now?

He glanced at his little brother and was surprised to see a smile spread across Asher's face. "They're back!" he pointed.

Mason turned toward the open sea. "Who?" He looked for another boat—hopefully a *big* one they would all fit into. Instead, he saw something silver streak across the water. Fins!

"They're coming to help us," Asher announced, as if he was certain of it. "I knew they'd be back!"

Mason felt a flutter of hope, too.

"But what can they do?" asked Luna. "Dolphin's Grace isn't going to get us all the way home."

Asher's face fell, but only for a moment. "They'll help us," he said again, jutting his jaw forward. "I know they will."

As Simon soared out of the water, his scarred fin rising toward the sky, the others followed. Squeaky chattered a friendly hello before diving back down.

"They're rocking the boat!" Luna said, hugging the edge as water lapped in.

Mason felt the water splash into his lap, but he couldn't tear his eyes away from the water. He'd just spotted something—something orange as a pumpkin—floating below the surface. Then a snout forced the object up, into the morning light.

"Your backpack!" Mason cried, jumping up so fast he nearly toppled out of the waterlogged boat.

Luna whirled around—and yelped with joy. "Yes!" she cried. "Thank you, Slugger!"

She reached over the edge of the boat so far, she lost her paddle. But she caught the strap of her backpack and lugged it into the boat. "Let's drink the potions right away," she said. "Because in a few seconds, we— and this boat—are going down."

She almost seems happy about that, Mason realized. Luna always seemed happiest in the water, as if she were a fish herself—at least when she had her potions.

Then he felt a jolt of happiness, too. If Luna had her potions back, she could heal his shoulder!

"Do you have potion of healing?" he cried, nearly grabbing the pack from her and searching himself.

Luna nodded, but as she pulled out the bottle, her face drooped. She held the bottle upside down—the *empty* bottle. "I used it all fighting the spider jockeys, remember?"

Mason struggled to recall. "No, you fought them with lingering potion," he said. "Lingering potion of harming!"

She shook her head. "Potion of harming doesn't harm undead mobs," she said. "Potion of healing does." Her shoulders slumped. "I'm sorry."

Mason blew out his breath. "Never mind," he said. "At least we have the other potions." But his shoulder ached at the thought of swimming all the way home. Even potion of swiftness wasn't going to take away the pain.

He made sure Asher drank each potion first, and then he took a few sips of his own. All the potions were getting low now—the rainbow of colorful liquids sloshed way below the midway marks on Luna's bottles. Would there be enough to get them home?

He didn't have long to wonder. The boat was disappearing beneath him, sucked downward by the weight of the water and the tug of the ocean floor.

"Dive!" Luna cried.

Mason's dive felt like more of a tumble. Soon, though, he was swimming. And seeing more clearly. And kicking quickly, as potion of swiftness began to take effect.

We have so far to go. Mason remembered the journey they'd made to find Asher. *Will I make it?*

He swallowed hard. *I have to try.* With a strong kick, he took off, keeping his sights set on the blur of his brother's green T-shirt ahead.

*   *   *

They had reached the ocean monument when Luna's potion of swiftness ran out. She held the bottle upside down in the water and shrugged.

It could be worse, Mason knew. It could have been potion of water breathing—the one they couldn't survive without down here.

But without potion of swiftness, his body felt so heavy. And slow.

Luna and Asher swam ahead, circling back now and then to check on Mason. He tried to smile to show them he was doing just fine. *But I'm not!* he wanted to cry. *I'm tired, and my shoulder is on fire. And home still seems so far away.*

Luna led them upward, high above the monument, as if she knew that Mason couldn't survive a battle with a guardian right now. Or with a drowned.

But swimming straight up was a struggle. Mason's body longed to go forward, to keep moving toward home instead of having to veer around the giant prismarine building below.

When he reached the surface, he popped his head out of the water for just a moment, savoring a breath of fresh air.

Luna surfaced beside him. "What is it?" she asked. "What can I do?"

Mason shook his head sadly. "Nothing," he said. "I just don't know . . . if I can make it."

The words hung between them like a lingering potion. Luna turned her head side to side, looking for a place where they could rest.

Then Mason heard the chirps of a worried dolphin. The fins were coming back now, all five of them in a straight line. They began to circle him, squeaking and squealing, as if trying to encourage him.

"I can't!" he said. "It's too far!"

Happy surfaced beside him, leaping so close that Mason could see the dolphin's smiling snout and feel the water droplets spraying off its side.

Then another leaped on Mason's other side. Was it Simon, their fearless leader? Yes. His scarred fin cut through the water, a reminder to Mason that the dolphin had seen hard times too—and survived.

Mason suddenly felt a wave surge beneath him, as if a third dolphin were pushing him forward. But it wasn't a dolphin. And it wasn't a swell of water.

What is it? Mason wondered.

As his body soared forward through the waves, he suddenly knew.

Dolphin's Grace. They gave me Dolphin's Grace!

Finally, finally, *finally* the dolphins trusted him enough to invite him to swim with them. Mason's strokes came easily now. He zoomed past Luna, watching the ocean monument slide beneath him.

A few seconds later, the effect wore off, but Mason had swum so far! When the effect wore off, Mason didn't even care.

I can keep going, he knew now. *Asher was right. The dolphins will help us get home!*

*   *   *

When the light of the conduit finally came into view, Mason swam toward it with everything he had. He passed Luna, who had paused to say hello to Edward the Squid. When Mason reached Asher's side, they swam together toward the beacon of light ahead.

The conduit was just how they'd left it—the blocks untouched, and the blue orb spinning round and round. Mason slid his hand across a smooth block of prismarine. Then he swam past the conduit toward the glass house beyond. Toward *home.*

Asher dove in front of him and waved his hand.

What? Mason studied his brother's freckled face.

Asher reached deep into his pocket and pulled something out—a handful of prismarine crystals. He held them out toward Mason like an offering until one began to float away.

Are those from the treasure chest? Mason wondered. *Asher left behind the diamond and the TNT, but he brought the crystals?*

Mason shook his head in wonder. It looked as if Asher was going to make good on his promise to craft a sea lantern, a block that would help Mason complete that last ring around the conduit and make it even more powerful.

He grinned and gave his brother a thumbs-up.

As Asher held up one of the crystals, catching the light of the conduit, something squeaked overhead. Slugger dove low beside Asher and nudged the crystal with his square snout. Mason glanced up and saw the rest of the pod of dolphins swimming high above, too, enjoying the light and safety of the conduit.

As he left his brother behind, playing a game of catch with Slugger, Mason smiled. They *would* make the conduit bigger and better one day soon. Maybe the protective light would reach all the way to the bubble column.

But there's an entire ocean beyond that column. And we can explore that, too, Mason thought. *Now that we have a few finned friends to help us.*

Squeaky chirped overhead as if to say, *You do.*